LISTENING TO
CATNIP

LISTENING TO CATNIP

STORIES FROM A CATANALYST'S COUCH

DR. SIGMUND F. WINNICAT
WITH CAMILLE SMITH

Carroll & Graf Publishers, Inc.
New York

First edition 1996

Carroll & Graf Publishers, Inc.
260 Fifth Avenue
New York, NY 10001

ISBN 0-7867-0357-1

Library of Congress Cataloging-in-Publication Data are available.

Manufactured in the United States of America.

To all my patients, and to my
favorite domesticated humans.
—S. F. W.

To all the cats who have domesticated me,
and to Forrest, my favorite human.
—C. S.

ACKNOWLEDGMENTS

I am grateful to many friends and colleagues—categories that often overlap—for tolerating my incessant requests to read yet another cat story, and for their astute and encouraging comments. Extra thanks to Betty Duskin for Paris, Helen Mazurek and Wendy Lesser for fax appreciation, Bill Patrick for the conception, and Margot Livesey for expert literary midwifery. And to several Smiths and Smith-Zurawskis, especially Marla, Emily, Nic, Lindsey, and Chris, for laughing in all the right places.

—C. S.

CONTENTS

INTRODUCTION

A catanalyst's time is seldom his own. Late one evening, while I was bathing in the middle of the bed my pet humans think of as theirs, I heard my cat door open and close. It seemed I had company. Reluctantly suspending my ablutions, I swallowed the strands of fur that had caught in my teeth and went into my office.

At first no one was visible. Casting my gaze around the room, I finally found my midnight visitor huddled behind the couch. A small-boned Abyssinian male, wild-eyed and shivering.

I approached hospitably, only to be met with raised hackles and sharp hisses. Quickly I retreated to the center of the room and resumed my toilette, taking care not to look directly at the newcomer. This classic catanalyst's ploy proved successful. As I licked between the toes of my right front paw, the tawny stranger emerged from his hiding place and sidled toward me.

Outwardly concentrating on my toes, I let him creep closer. My right front paw was becoming unprecedentedly clean. At long last I felt the tickle of whiskers against my flank and heard a tentative sniffing.

It was time to meet his eyes. They were a bright copper, slitted with suspicion at first but gradually widening as he relaxed. Soon I was able to sniff him in my turn and even bat at his tail with my immaculate paw. And soon after that my newest patient was on the couch instead of behind it, and I was listening intently to his hoarse mews as he explained why he needed my help.

* * *

Why *do* patients enter catanalysis? Their reasons are as varied as the hairs in a tortoiseshell's coat. Perhaps they spent their kittenhood in a dysfunctional litter. Perhaps they were an only kitten, or, at the opposite extreme, the last of a litter of eleven, one more mouth than a mamacat is biologically equipped to feed. Perhaps humans have destroyed their self-esteem with abusive words like "No!" and "Bad cat!" They may suffer from a stalking disability or from hypercativity, or they may be equilibrially challenged and incapable of landing on their feet.

Whatever brings them into treatment, most patients have one problem in common: difficulties with daydreaming. Such difficulties, which I call Daydreaming Disorders, are reaching epidemic proportions in feline society today. Ironically enough, it is one of our greatest accomplishments—our successful domestication of humans—that makes us vulnerable to this thoroughly modern malaise.

Relatively few of our species, in this prosperous age,

live the feral life of our ancestors, in which ever-present danger and the need to hunt for food left little time for daydreaming. Instead, many of us now rely on our pet humans to open cans of catfood, and spend our days and nights inside the safe dwellings known, in the technical terminology of my profession, as Good Homes. Life in such homes is the goal of most contemporary cats; we may never see a return of the golden age of ancient Egypt, when our forecats were worshiped, but living with a devoted human can come close.

Good Homes, however, also have their pitfalls. As we learned from Kitty Friedan's landmark work *The Feline Mystique*, the confinement and lack of stimulation in such environments, along with the negative self-image of being "just a housecat," can seriously threaten felinemotional health.

Those housecats who triumph over this threat and thrive in their Good Homes possess a capacity for active imagination; that is, they are able to transport themselves to other places and other times through daydreams. This talent of our species is expressed in the well-known adage concerning the proverbial allotment of lives per cat: "A daydream in time saves nine."*

If you believe you suffer from a Daydreaming Disorder, do not despair; with skilled professional help you

* For more about Nine Lives, the truncated form of immortality promised by certain feline cults, see *Curiosity Killed the Cat—But Not to Worry: A First-Paw Account of My Multiple Cathoods,* by Shirley MacCat (Catmandu: Hot Tin Roof Press, 1986).

can learn to guide your fantasies in healthy directions. Traditionally, the learning has required years of catanalysis, often several sessions per week—a commitment difficult to squeeze into schedules already crammed with napping and eating. In recent years, however, a far less time-consuming method of treatment has come into fashion. Its basis is not so much psycatlogical as pharmacatlogical—not the traditional long-term "meowing cure," but the use of medication.

* * *

For some time now, in my practice, I have explored the therapeutic use of *Nepeta cataria,* commonly called catnip. This plant has a long and varied history, going back at least as far as ancient Egypt. (Feline scholars have deciphered hieroglyphics depicting the Great Sphinx, under the influence of the sacred herb, rolling in the desert sand with a gleeful expression.) Today, even as it gains acceptance as a catanalytic tool, it is most widely used as a recreational drug. In my youth it was considered illicit, and I recall several occasions when alley cats surreptitiously offered it to me on the street. With a typical catolescent need to act cool, I accepted—but I did not inhale.

Later, when carefully calibrated doses of catnip were found to be medicinally useful, I regretted my youthful hesitancy. I realized that experience with the drug would have heightened my consciousness—my consciousness, that is, of how to help my patients. Eventually I did self-administer it a number of times (precisely how many I cannot say; my memories of those occasions are oddly vague) before prescribing it for anyone else.

Catnip therapy has proved remarkably successful. In spite of this success, however—or perhaps precisely because of it—I retain some misgivings about the use of drugs in catanalysis. When we discover a new method of treatment, the treatment itself alters our definitions of what should be treated. In the present case, we *listen to catnip* and are changed by what we hear.*

Precisely how to listen is a matter of dispute in catanalytic circles. On the one paw, the flamboyant Hungarian colorpoint Dr. Sandy Furrenczi recommends a state-of-the-art procedure involving headphones and digital technology. On another paw, the distinguished Swiss tabby Dr. Curly Jung proposes listening with a collective ear—a notion which makes my own quite individual auditory organs twitch in skeptical irritation (a sensation not unlike that of an infestation of ear mites). On the fourth and final paw,† the method I myself have found most effective is to lie down and rub one's ears directly in the herb, preferably while batting at a companion or, if alone, chasing one's tail.

What does it mean to listen to catnip? Perhaps I may draw an analogy to the way the gullible humans in the

* It is one thing to listen to the drug, of course, and quite another to understand what it says. For this reason, I am a strong advocate of mandatory catnip-language classes as a part of catanalytic training.

† The third paw I shall leave for Mrs. Meownie Klein, whose methods of listening deserve a book of their own.

Garden of Eden listened to the serpent as it tempted them with the fruit of the Tree of Knowledge.* Like the serpent, the drug insinuates that we lack knowledge—specifically, that we have failed to recognize certain felinemotional conditions as disorders that should be treated.

It is our response to this message that prompts my misgivings. Many Daydreaming Disorders, such as the Dull Daydreaming of my patients Abby and Slade (see Chapter 3), were considered quite normal before my profession discovered catnip therapy. Today, because we have learned how to tinker with feline fantasies, we define many such fantasies as *in need of* tinkering. As when scratching to relieve a flea bite only inflames it further, the cure creates the disease.

Notwithstanding these doubts, I must confess that I have listened to catnip as attentively as anyone in my field. Those of my colleagues who oppose catnip therapy, on the grounds that the disorders it treats were not defined *as* disorders until catanalysts became interested in the drug, would do well to consider the ultimate implications of their argument. Our entire profession, in fact, exists to treat disorders that were not so defined until the tenets of catanalysis sprang full blown, like a brilliant theoretical hairball, from the throat of our es-

* Had Adam and Eve allowed the Garden cats to follow their instinct and pounce on the serpent, both cats and humans would still reside in Eden. Thus to this day, to atone for their disrespect for feline wisdom, humans are kept as pets by our species.

teemed founder, the Viennese longhair Papa Sigmund. Shall we, Papa's descendcats, argue away the *raison d'être* of our own endeavors? I trust we shall not succumb to such a typically human folly.*

* Humans, too, are said to listen to certain drugs. In the case of a medication known as Prozac, apparently some not only listen but also talk back. Oh, to be a flea on the wall during these discussions!

Oh, brave new world, that has such potions in't!
—W. Shakestail

LISTENING TO
CATNIP

1

FELIX THE CATANALYSAND

Felix (not his real name), a tabby in middle cathood, came to catanalysis complaining of depression. His appearance and manner were consistent with that diagnosis: ears and whiskers limp, tail dragging behind him, fur drab and ungroomed. I suspected, however, that when not listless and having a bad fur day he must be pawsome: white whiskers contrasting with a gray-striped coat of medium length; a wedge-shaped face marred only by its hangcat expression. In spite of his suffering I sensed his potential to be a charming and active member of society—in technical terms, a real pussycat.

After we sniffed each other politely on my office rug, I asked Felix to make himself comfortable in a grocery bag on the couch. Any catanalyst worth his or her kibble aims to create, in the catanalytic setting, a so-called holding environment, in which the patient feels safe. Reclining inside a bag—an object that exists solely for holding—encourages my catanalysands to relax and let their fur down.* Felix's story, as he mewed it to me, was a typical one—insofar as any individual's life story can be at once typical and unique. Born at a cattery, one of a set of quintuplets, he had competed with his littermates from birth for their mama's milk, for the touch of her grooming tongue, for room to curl up against her belly to be lulled to sleep by her purr.

When hardly old enough to open his eyes, Felix had learned from a catty cousin that the long-haired black tom he thought of as his father was, indeed, his father—but was also his older brother. As so often happens when, in a reversal of the natural order of things, humans presume to control feline lives, his mamacat had been bred to one of her own sons.

Imagine the impact of this revelation on the sensitive kitten. The competing feelings of despair and hope: despair of ever comprehending his family tree (if his brother mated for life with their mama, would that make Felix her son or her brother-in-law?), contending with the hope, which members of the human branch of my profession call oedipal, that one day he might take his father/brother's place in the mamacat's affections.† Had the young Felix known of the Operation humans had in

* I prefer paper bags to the alternative proposed by some catanalysts and many grocery clerks: see my article "Paper or Plastic?" *Annals of Therapeutic Bagology* (1994).

† I have long argued that feline mental health professionals should pay more attention to the human legend of Oedipus. See my "Oedipuss and Jocatsa: Cataclysmic Consanguinity Among Hellenic Felines," *Journal of Inadvertent Inbreeding* (1990).

store for him, which they called "getting fixed," his despair would undoubtedly have predominated.

Felix's story went on to include his weaning, his discovery of tuna and other delicacies as substitutes for mama's milk, the shock of being sent away from his family to live with a human, the first trip to the veterinarian, and then the Operation. When he came to me he had been "fixed" for more than a year and had recovered well. He had come to care for his pet human, an adult female called Georgia, and to enjoy the touch of her furless paw almost as much as he had once loved the caress of his mamacat's rough tongue.

Nevertheless, Felix was depressed.

* * *

Of course I did not simply take the patient's word for it. I administered the standard questionnaire concerning the symptoms of depression, and the diagnosis was incontestable. He had trouble sleeping through the day, and often awoke in midafternoon feeling restless but unable to think of anything to do. At night he was often too exhausted to keep vigil at the mousehole under the kitchen sink. If a moth or a mosquito entered the house through the holes that, in happier times, Felix had cleverly made in the window screens, he watched passively as it flew around the room, making no attempt to catch it. He lacked the energy to unwind Georgia's toilet paper from its roll, and once or twice he had even failed to finish his dinner.

In addition to this clear evidence of depression, Felix

showed signs of the disorder technically known as "uptight." The markings on his coat were so constricted by his felineurosis as to resemble pinstripes and a necktie rather than normal tabby stripes. Combined with his generally neglected appearance, they called to mind certain types more often found among humans than among cats—perhaps a gone-to-seed accountant or a disbarred attorney.

Even more alarming than this resemblance to humans was Felix's loss of the ability to daydream.* Like any normal cat who lives mostly indoors, he spent many hours of each twenty-four staring through the window at the world outside. Unlike normal cats, however, as he stared he experienced no fantasies whatsoever. A passing squirrel was merely a squirrel, a falling leaf just a leaf, even a bird only its feathered self.

When, in our first session, I asked Felix how he had spent recent sleepless afternoons, this was his answer:

> Let's see, yesterday I counted 156 leaves drifting past the window before I took a break to claw the sofa. Mostly maple, I'd say 87 percent, but a few from the oak next door. Seventeen sparrows flew by early on, followed by five pigeons and two chickadees around sunset. No squirrels at all, and I kept a close watch, only looked away once, when

* My critics, Dr. Furrenczi in particular, have claimed that "daydreaming" is a misleading term given the nocturnal nature of our species. The term, however, has been widely used by catanalysts ever since Papa Sigmund published his purrspicacious work *The Interpretation of Daydreams.*

my, um, you know . . . when the . . . when the place under my tail needed licking. Well. Except for the squirrels, these are typical numbers for this time of year.

However admirable his accounting skills (and however anal his preoccupations), Felix was in danger of severe and lasting *Daydream Deprivation*—a condition from which few cats have ever recovered.*

* * *

I first offered Felix catnip during our second session. As I knew then from the pioneering work of Dr. Timousy Leary and know now from my own observations, response to the drug varies so extremely from patient to patient that it is best administered under close supervision. A small percentage of patients cannot tolerate it at all, and fall into the life-threatening state known as the catniption fit.

When Felix sniffed the small mound of dried herb I had placed on the couch, he catapulted from his paper bag and rolled in the medication. Then, without warning, he leaped upon me and bit my left ear.

Obviously I could not continue to supervise Felix quite so closely: technically speaking, the patient had rubbed my fur the wrong way. In the catanalytic trans-

* An exception is the smooth-meowed Bing Catby, who underwent treatment for this disorder at the Catty Ford Center and achieved at least a partial recovery, as evidenced by his subsequent fame for "Daydreaming of a White Christmas."

ference, he was confusing me with someone from his fuzzy past. I have always understood the importance of transference, and just then I judged it prudent to transfer myself to another room.

Despite this inauspicious beginning, I followed Dr. Leary's precepts and persevered with the treatment. At Felix's next visit I administered a smaller dose and took the precaution of positioning myself on top of my office bookshelves. After briefly burrowing under a cushion on the couch, Felix was able to return to the bag and resume the session.

The therapeutic effect of the medication was remarkable and almost immediate. Felix regained his ability to daydream. A squirrel outside the window was no longer merely a squirrel but prey to be pursued by Felix the Fierce. Falling leaves were transformed into attacking creatures from which Felix would rescue himself and Georgia. At night the lights of passing automobiles, which had barely attracted his notice before his treatment, became the glowing eyes of dragons, or phasers from space ships piloted by alien rodents. In every case Felix the Fierce was there to save the day.

Simultaneously with this resurgence of fantasy activity, other aspects of Felix's life returned to normal. His fur regained its shine and his markings relaxed into true tabby stripes so that he no longer resembled a seedy accountant or any other sort of human. He could now sleep all day long. At night he had boundless energy and spent hours hunting mousies or guarding the house against space ships and dragons. He made short work of

any insect misguided enough to enter the house through his holes in the screen—and he even showed a healthy initiative by enlarging the holes. Once again Georgia had to roll up the toilet paper every morning, and Felix ate with a vigorous appetite.

* * *

Perhaps it will be useful to quote Felix's account of the afternoon following his second dose of catnip:

> I was just sitting on the kitchen table, kind of looking out the window, watching for squirrels. Then I saw them. Squirrels—not! They came marching across the windowsill, an army of them. Ugly things—not very big, but definitely dangerous. No fur, lumpy black bodies, things like starched whiskers waving around their heads—antennae, I think they're called—and two extra legs each! If I hadn't been there, well, what would have happened? I hate to think. Georgia had left for work in a hurry as usual, and the bread and jam were sitting on the table, open targets.
>
> I waited. Didn't move even a hair—well, not counting the tip of my tail, which kept jerking around on its own. When they got so close I could see the whites of their eyes—except that there wasn't any white in their eyes, but then we cats don't have white in our eyes either, so why do we use that expression? Kind of interesting, when you think about it. It's like my brother Daddy used to say—we all listen to humans too much.

Here, as so often happens in catanalysis, the patient digressed, and the digression was significant. Felix, quite inadvertently, revealed that he had made remarkable progress toward resolution of his oedipal problems. His acceptance of his dual relationship with the tom he called Daddy seemed nearly complete.

I shall let him finish recounting his daydream:

Well. When those invaders got close I just reached out one paw and stomped it down on their leaders. Squished five with one blow! After that it was easy—a few more swipes with my paw, and the survivors named me Destroyer and turned tail—except that they didn't really have tails, come to think of it—and marched back out the window.

Next thing I knew I was running all through the house and straight up the bedroom curtains! Had to knock over an asparagus fern and roll in the dirt just to work off my energy. The thing is, after I terrorized them into retreating I was, you know, sort of sorry to see them go. Not every day I get to fight an army.

I got back on the table and watched the window the rest of the day—didn't even nap. If Georgia only knew how much I do for her, she'd get over her hissy-fit about that asparagus fern.

Although it might be argued (and has been, at length, by Dr. Furrenczi) that the content of Felix's catnip-influenced daydreams does not indicate the presence of mature felinego defenses, I myself judged his treatment a success. I tapered the dose of medication and found that soon he could do without catnip altogether. His daydreams became increasingly vivid, his fur retained its elegance—and his preoccupations remained anal only in the literal way so vital to feline hygiene.

His depression showed no signs of recurring. Indeed, in a surge of creativity, he invented new games to entertain his pet, such as Scatter the Clean Laundry, a variation of this called Steal the Dirty Socks, and his own favorite, Hide the Remote Control.

We agreed to terminate the catanalysis. The patient was cured—to put it in technical terms, the cat was out of the bag.

2

PUFF'S VIRTUAL REALITY

Felix's recovery intensified my interest in the psycatherapeutic potential of catnip. It also strengthened my conviction that daydreaming is crucial to felinemotional well-being.

I have elected to call healthy, life-enhancing daydreams *Virtual Adventures*. Perhaps the story of another of my patients, one who suffered not from Daydream Deprivation but from *Daydream Misdirection,* will clarify the concept.

I first saw the patient I shall call Puff, a petite calico in early middle cathood, shortly after she had been rescued from a shelter by a human family who offered her a Good Home. The period of homelessness preceding her stay in the shelter had left its marks: some literal ones, such as the nick in one ear caused by the claw of an alley cat in a dispute over a scrap of food; others more elusive, such as her masochistic attraction to feral toms.

Life in the shelter itself had been nothing to purr about. Safe from the depredations of street life, dining on kibble rather than rodents and scraps, even freed of

her attraction to abusive males by the Operation provided at the shelter, she nevertheless lived in a cage, and the cage was surrounded by other cages inhabited by other cats—and even dogs! Whenever a staff member attempted to stroke her fur, Puff would crouch at the back of her prison and hiss. The rest of the time she lay on the floor of the cage in a state of catatonia.

Into this inhospitable environment came humans, from time to time, to apply for the position of pet to a cat or—quite inexplicably—to a dog.* For several days all the applicants passed Puff's cage without a second glance; her lack of affect discouraged them from attempting to become her pets.

Then one morning Puff noticed a family of three humans walking down the aisle between the cages. The smallest of the three, a yellow-haired male of about six human years, caught her attention. Like so many young members of his species, he was adorable, and his wide-eyed interest was so appealing that Puff, in spite of her catanomie, wanted him for her own. The little boy reached a furless paw through the bars of the cage, and Puff rubbed her head against it and to her own surprise remembered how to purr. Shortly thereafter the family

* The origins of the division of humans into so-called Cat People and Dog People are lost in precatstory. We know that humans became pets to cats as a result of Adam and Eve's disrespectful behavior in the Garden of Eden; similarly, the bond of certain humans with dogs may have begun with Cain and Abel. As Cain (or Canine) was condemned to wander the earth, so Dog People must roam long distances holding leashes and carrying pooper scoopers, in that mystifying doggy custom known as Walkies.

applied to be adopted as her pets: Puff's affectionate affect, in effect, affected the course of her life.

* * *

In many ways Puff's story is an example of the classic catanalytic concept known as Happily Ever After. She acquired a Good Home, the goal for which so many of us strive, and in the end she did find happiness. But the transition was not entirely easy. Now loved and pampered, especially by the young male human called Davy, Puff nevertheless continued to suffer from mild depression. She came to me after several weeks in her new abode.

When she was settled in the bag I asked about her daydreams. As she recounted them the root of her disorder became apparent. She had an active fantasy life, but the fantasies were negative. Automobiles passing in the street below her pets' apartment became garbage trucks, threatening to crush her to death or to steal the garbage before she could search it for food. Pedestrians on the sidewalks were angry mobs from medieval times, accusing innocent cats of consorting with human witches. The stimuli were neutral enough, but Puff *misdirected* them into terrifying fantasies.

An example from an early session may be helpful:

> Oh, Doctor, I have always depended on the kindness of humans. And yet humans can be so unkind.
>
> I don't mean Davy, of course, Davy is a darling

> boy, and such a comfortable size compared to those huge tall ones. He knows a lot, too, for a pet. Poetry, he knows wonderful poetry. Every night at bedtime his mama reads poems to him, and I snuggle at the foot of his bed and listen. Have you heard the one about the Cat in the Hat? "Look at me, look at me, look at me now! It's fun to have fun, but you have to know how!"

The lines Puff quoted, by a human with the whimsical name Dr. Seuss, might be taken as a metaphor for the entire endeavor of catanalysis: Our patients come to us because they are unable to have fun, and by giving them our undivided attention ("Look at [and listen to] me now!") we help them learn how.

Puff continued:

> But those other humans, the ones in the streets, the huge tall ones! I saw two of them get out of some big black car, like a gigantic bug, this morning, and my fur stuck out in all directions. Then suddenly, I don't know how it happened, I was out in the street too and they had noticed me. When they came closer I saw that they were with a—I can hardly bear to say it—they were with a DOG.
>
> Oh, Doctor, you know how I long for the old days on the plantation, the big house with the beautiful columns—that's the human word for tall scratching posts—across the front porch. You know about the cruel, cruel hounds who kept me up a tree until I nearly starved, then chased me off the land my family had lived on forever. You know how that paw-to-mouth existence made me swear I'd never be hungry again. You know how I cried for my mama

and my littermates, especially my sister Stella, when I was lost in the city, so far from home. And you know what happened when I found Stella with that low-class tomcat Brando Catalski.

I suspected that Puff's account of her early life involved a certain exaggeration; as all catanalysts know, memories themselves, particularly memories of one's kittenhood, are often a form of Virtual Reality. But it was verifiable that she and her littermates, including a sister called Stella, had been born in a rural setting, and that Puff had been exiled from her home at an early age by a mixed-species gang of canine and human persecutors.

Her tone as she related her story was somewhat flirtatious, and once she leaned forward out of the bag to lick my face. It seemed her Operation had not entirely subdued certain of her instincts. I could only assume the transference was at work. When I offered no response, she sniffed at my whiskers for a moment—making me hope the tartar-control treats I had chewed before the session had removed the odor of my liver-and-beef-bits breakfast—then tucked her paws neatly beneath her and spoke again.

A kitty does what she must to live, you know. No one could say I liked digging through Dumpsters for my meals. And all those toms. But I survived.

This morning, though, when that monster, that DOG came toward me, it brought it all back. The dog was ten times my size, and its huge tall pets were even bigger. They were running after me, faster and faster. I had no place to hide. It was even worse than that time Stella went off to have her kittens and left me alone with Brando Catalski. I just knew my time had come. I'd lost the family plantation so long ago, and now I was going to lose my life!

Puff sank back into the bag with a dramatic sigh. Although living in perfect safety with a family of Cat People—who would protect her from any threatening Dog People, let alone dogs—she was in the grip of *Virtual Traumas,* which echoed the bad experiences of her early life. The goal of her treatment would be to replace her Virtual Traumas with Virtual Adventures.

* * *

I administered catnip at our third session, and as in Felix's case the effects were impressive. By the fourth time I saw Puff her whiskers slanted upward, her tail formed a jaunty snow-white curve, and she reported looking forward to her daydreams. "Well fiddle-de-dee, Doctor," she confided. "If anything bothers me, I just tell myself, 'I'll think about it tomorrow. After all, tomorrow is another daydream.' "

In her new and improved fantasies, automobiles might be coaches bearing beautiful cats to a ball on a moonlit night, or perhaps metal monsters from which Puff the Warrior Queen would save her beloved city. Human pedestrians became adoring crowds cheering Queen Puff for rescuing them. In a particularly striking

example—perhaps prompted by one of young Davy's favorite poems—Puff formed a partnership with an owl, and the two of them went to sea in a beautiful pea-green catamaran.*

These were Virtual Adventures indeed—and another victory for pharmacatherapy. Without catnip, Puff might never have been able to fight her way out of the paper bag.

* Dr. Furrenczi, missing the point as usual, has argued that under my care Puff lost touch with reality altogether. It is basic to my theory that, particularly for housebound cats, losing touch with reality *temporarily* is vital to mental health.

3

ABBY AND SLADE

Not all my patients have come to me through the usual channels, such as referral from general catpractitioners or curiosity about what lies behind my cat door. For example, I happened upon two catanalysands while exercising in my neighborhood.

Having no appointments one morning, I left the house and spent a vigorous hour climbing trees and dashing from bush to bush in pursuit of squirrels. (My purrsonal trainer is an advocate of cross-training: alternating tree climbing with prey chasing. She recommends this sort of exercise daily except in inclement weather, when she allows me to substitute racing up and down stairs and streaking through the house attempting to trip my pets.)

While crouched under a rhododendron bush watching a squirrel gorge himself at one of those all-you-can-eat platforms that humans call birdfeeders, I sensed that I, too, was being observed. Through a window of a nearby house, two plump, bored-looking catolescents were staring at me.

I signaled to them by leaping onto the birdfeeder. (The squirrel, erroneously assuming I was still cross-

training, had decamped.) The young cats widened their eyes and extended their tails in welcome. After the usual greetings—although the screen on their window inhibited the customary mutual sniffing—I identified myself as a catanalyst and, prompted by my conviction that anyone in the throes of catolescence is likely to be in felinemotional distress, asked if they had access to grocery bags.

* * *

Abby and Slade (they have permitted the use of their real names) were twins who had been together since birth. Their twinship was not identical; indeed, their looks supported the theory that kittens in the same litter may have different fathers (they claimed never to have questioned their mamacat about this). Abby was a blue-eyed longhair with the coloring and markings of a blue-point Himalayan; Slade a gray shorthair with gold eyes and a smooth and sculptural, if rotund, silhouette. Their relationship did show in their faces, identical triangles under their very different fur, and in the color of Abby's markings, which matched Slade's charcoal shade. Both, to put it tactfully, looked extremely well-fed—although Abby's girth may have been somewhat exaggerated by the length of her coat.

They had been a litter of two, born into a family of seven cats who shared one pet human, an adult female who answered to the name Donna. Aware that when the cat-to-pet ratio reaches such a high level a household is in danger of ceasing to be a Good Home, their relatives had commissioned Donna to find the kittens other accommodation.* When old enough to leave their mama, the twins had traveled by cat carrier to the house they would share with their new pets, a pair of adult humans.

This ratio—one to one—was pleasing to all. The new pets seemed to understand what was expected of them and needed only minimal training. They provided delectable food (perhaps too much of it), clean litter, warm bodies to sleep with at night, recreational exercise, and as much stroking as Abby and Slade would allow. They wisely put the kittens at the center of the household, consulting them before making any important decisions, such as what ornaments to hang on the Christmas tree or whether to throw out the liquid from a newly opened can of tuna.

* * *

In our first conversation it became apparent that Abby and Slade enjoyed the usual feline pleasures: to eat, to sleep, perchance to daydream. But aye, there was the rub—and it did not smooth the fur in a comfortable direction. Their daydreams, as they recounted them, evoked in me a most uncatanalytic boredom. The end of the session seemed a consummation devoutly to be wished. My thoughts wandered to what I might find in my food dish at dinnertime; I experienced a sharp crav-

* The critical impact of cat-to-pet ratios on feline mental health has spawned the One Cat, One Pet movement, with its well-known slogan "A Lap for Every Cat, and a Cat in Every Lap."

ing for Salmon Supreme. My rigorous training, however, enabled me to focus on my patients despite these impulses, and soon I was able to categorize Abby and Slade's fantasies by their content, as shown in the following table:*

Content of Daydream	*Share of Total Daydreaming*
Their most recent meal	49%
Their next meal	49%
Quests to find valuable household items on which to sharpen their claws	1%
The pursuit of small rodents with which to play Spanish Inquisition	1%

Although listening to the twins' calorie-laden fantasies had made my whiskers droop with ennui, these statistics restored my scientific appetite.† Here was a disorder I had not encountered before, not even in catanalytic text-

* For this rigorously scientific method of categorizing daydreams I am indebted to a human economist, P. Hennessy, a highly regarded pet of some of my European colleagues.

† I must point out that Dr. Furrenczi's latest insinuation, that in my quantitative work I share certain undesirable characteristics with Felix in his pinstriped stage, amounts to an ad catinem attack that demeans catanalysis in general.

books: *Daydreaming Dullness.* Like any doctor confronted with a new challenge, I felt my tail twitch and my ears stand fully erect. Given my success with earlier patients like Felix and Puff, I immediately thought of Abby and Slade as candidates for catnip therapy.

Critics of psycatpharmacology have hissed, perhaps with some justification, that nothing in this first session indicated that these patients needed treatment of *any* kind. Their fantasy profile was within the normal range for well-adjusted housecats. (By well-adjusted, of course, I mean only mildly felineurotic—for what cat among us entirely lacks neurosis? Indeed, I have heard learned colleagues speculate that a cat totally without neurosis would be a gerbil.)

What is more, Abby and Slade's emphasis on food resembled that of many geniuses from the history of our species. If a catanalyst had diagnosed Mousel Proust's food-centered daydreams as dull, my colleagues growled, would feline civilization have been deprived of his masterpiece, *Remembrance of Repasts Past?* The only reason I proposed treating Abby and Slade at all, according to this view, was that I had *listened to catnip*—listened as it whispered in my ear that some types of daydreams were "healthier" than others.

* * *

Because I put my patients' well-being ahead of all other considerations—and not, as Dr. Furrenczi has asserted, because I had catnip coming out my ears—I chose to go ahead with Abby and Slade's treatment. It boded well that the twins lived in a house with many windows looking out on good material for fantasy: the birdfeeding platform, a garden with trees and bushes, a suburban street. And, they told me, one of the cabinets in the kitchen held a small box of catnip, which their pets offered to them on holidays for recreational use. This was fortunate, as they never left their house and the window between us made it difficult for me to supply them with the medication.*

As we planned their treatment, the issue of methodology arose. I would need to hear their daydreams in detail to determine the effectiveness of the drug. Inasmuch as communication through an open window was feasible only so long as the weather remained warm, the approach of a New England autumn threatened to curtail our sessions.

The solution was one surely undreamed of by Papa Sigmund, indeed one unknown to our forecats of even a generation ago. Abby and Slade's pets possessed a computer and subscribed to an on-line service. My pets, also, were equipped to travel what humans call the information superhighway.† Abby and Slade were blessed with

* It is rare, in this day and age, for members of my profession to make house calls. As a specialist in imagination and daydreaming, however, I find that my services are often most needed by cats who cannot visit my office. Cats who roam freely face many dangers unknown to their housebound fellows—but those very dangers make them less dependent on their imaginations to sustain their mental health.

† This phrase is an instance of the endearing human inability to accept new technology without clinging to images of the old: consider the horseless carriage, moving pictures, electronic mail, and the notebook

polydactyly (in the vernacular, extra toes or double paws), which enabled them to type with impressive speed—and of course they were experts at manipulating the mouse. The curious human custom of sleeping during the nocturnal hours provided excellent opportunities for surreptitious communication. We agreed that Abby and Slade would wait until their pets were safely abed, then connect to the on-line service and send me their daydreams as e-mail. While my own pets slumbered I would retrieve the messages and commit them to memory.* In the tradition of the silent catanalyst, I would send no responses.

As for the administration of catnip, the twins would have to see to it themselves—each supervising the other—once I had calibrated the dosage. Accordingly, I met them at the window on a day when their pets were absent. Abby demonstrated her considerable skill at cupboard opening by extracting the box of catnip from its cabinet and bringing it to the window seat. She placed it near the twin grocery bags she and Slade had dragged there before the session.

---

computer. See my "Transitional Anachronisms: A Metaphor for Humankind?" (unpublished catuscript).

* The American Catanalytic Association (ACA) recommends that we cats not use our pets' printers. It is deemed wise to conceal our level of technological sophistication—and indeed our ability to read. E-mail messages, after being read, are to be deleted or stored in a hidden directory. There is little danger that our pets will notice the extra charges for these messages, as both the on-line services and the telephone companies have devised billing systems so convoluted that only a cat could comprehend them.

On my instructions, Abby nudged the box until a small mound of catnip spilled onto the seat. I asked her to partake of the medication before her brother. She complied, sniffing delicately at the herb and rolling onto her back. However, while she lay supine, all four double paws waving in the air, Slade thrust her aside and stretched out in her place. He rolled over several times, then stood up, approached his sister in a slow, sidewise motion, and leaped upon her. As I watched in cat-analytic silence, he held her firmly with his front paws and pummeled her face with his strong hind feet.

Abby reciprocated—or perhaps I should say retaliated. In the rather misleading technical phrase, they fought like cats and dogs. To my trained eye their behavior beautifully typified the ambivalence of the sibling relationship: What littermates among us have not embraced fervently, the better to kick each other in the face?*

With this comforting reflection I brought the session to a close.

* * *

The following week the twins were willing to try the same dose of catnip a second time—indeed, Slade professed himself more than willing—but I could not permit this. The welfare of the patients is paramount: I revere the sacred principles of feline medicine ex-

* I have discussed this phenomenon more fully in "When Puss Comes to Shove," *Annals of Tooth and Claw* (1995).

pressed in the Hippocatic Oath. Accordingly, I directed Abby and Slade to cut the dosage in half, and to take it one at a time. Because of Slade's demonstrated difficulty with delayed gratification, he was to go first.

This second trial proceeded without untoward incident, except that Abby was seized by an acute attack of the mousies (a condition similar to what humans call the munchies)—a common side effect of the drug. We were forced to suspend the session while she opened a cupboard and clawed a hole in a bag of kibble. She offered to share, but Slade, now reclining on the floor and dreamily rubbing his face against the carpet, did not respond. As for me, the barrier created by the window screen saved me from having to choose between proper catanalytic behavior and the undeniably seductive smell of Tuna Delite.

After her snack, Abby revived Slade at my request—by the simple expedient of pouncing on him from the window seat and biting his throat—and we completed our treatment plan. The twins would send me their daydreams by e-mail. They wished to collaborate in writing the messages, and to take the time to shape their daydreams into stories.* Fearing collaboration would sacrifice spontaneity, however, I urged them to compose their messages individually. I also asked them to include

* In these ambitions Abby and Slade aspired to join a storytelling tradition that dates back at least as far as Geoffrey Mouser's famous *Catterbury Tails*. Literature is not my field, of course, but see my "A Flea in His Ear: Echoes of Catnip in Mouser's 'The Cat of Bath's Tail,' " *Journal of Literary Non Sequiturs* (1990).

some reference to the real-life context surrounding their fantasies.

So we agreed. I returned to my office to await what I fervently hoped would *not* be a reverie about past or future repasts.

4

LOW-FAT DAYDREAMING

I set up a directory in which to store incoming e-mail from Abby and Slade. I called it DOCWIN, knowing that if my pets happened to notice it listed in their file manager they would assume it was part of their Windows software.

From the first line of Slade's first transmission—a title his pretreatment self could not have created—I knew his fantasies had been transformed. The title was "Slade Saves the Neighborhood."

A normal morning. I was taking it easy in the window seat. My sister was giving herself a tongue shampoo on the oriental rug. Outside the window was the usual scene—rhododendron bushes and the street in front of our house.

Our pets, two nonpedigreed humans, were reading the newspaper over breakfast. The smaller pet was skimming the paper from front to back. The larger one seemed to be memorizing the sports section. Like I said, a normal morning.

The smaller pet spoke up. "Honey, it says here

that cats can't see colors, just black and white. They even *dream* in black and white."

The larger pet was staring at the baseball scores. "Mmm-hmm," he said.

The pets do have names, but Abby and I usually think of them in terms of size. Anyway, besides their real names, they answer to others like Honey and Cupcake. I mean, gag me with a wishbone! No way will you ever hear me call my sister Tuna or Tender Vittles.

The pets are cute, but not too bright. They seem to believe everything they read in the paper. Truth is, my dreams may not be exactly action-packed, but they're as colorful as poached salmon in dill sauce.

The opening of Slade's daydream reveals a healthy attitude toward his pets. For those of us who keep humans around the house, a sense of humor is essential. Without it we might become as earnest as dogs; we might even end up performing the species-inappropriate behavior known as "tricks." The proper humorous perspective enables us to train our pets while gently deflecting their amusing attempts to train us. Most cats easily maintain a salutary ascendancy over their humans; those few who do not suffer terrible shame, and many of them enter catanalysis.*

Slade's reference to salmon in dill sauce, juxtaposed with his comment about the lack of action in his

* For more on this rare affliction see my "Cats Who Purr Too Much: Learning to Bite the Hand That Feeds You," *Annals of Clinical Catology* (forthcoming).

dreams, is undoubtedly a response to my diagnosis of Daydreaming Dullness, a gentle way of teasing me. Such teasing is a sign of beginning recovery. I cannot overemphasize the importance of humor and play in felinemotional health: To quote once again the unusually wise human Dr. Seuss, "It's fun to have fun, but you have to know how."

A breeze made the rhododendron leaves wiggle and swish. The tip of my tail swished, too. Something was about to happen.

I heard it first, then saw it coming down the street—a huge monster. Its sides were a glaring yellow, with black markings that looked like this: GARBAGE.

The monster screeched to a halt in front of the house. Two humans climbed out of its sides, grabbed some big cans from the curb, and emptied them into its gigantic mouth. It chewed with a grinding roar that flattened my ears to my head.

I looked around for Abby. There she was, making herself as small as possible behind a houseplant. No surprise—my sister's a fierce hunter when she's in the mood, and she raves about Grimalkin Greer's felinist manifesto *The Feline Eunuch,** but fighting monsters has never been one of her hobbies. I was on my own.

I put on my trusty shades. Nothing like a disguise when you're on the prowl. One last look through the window, then I shut my eyes.

* Originally published by the University of Catifornia Press under the title *The Spayee.*

In keeping with the "suspension of disbelief"* required to enjoy a daydream to the fullest, Slade suppresses his ability to read so that he may fail to comprehend the identifying label written on his "monster." His method of making the transition between quotidian reality and Virtual Adventure is also worth comment. Unlike Puff, who fell into disturbing daydreams without any predictable transition, Slade employs a mechanism—the donning of a pair of dark eyeglasses—that allows him to enter the Virtual world when he chooses.

His choice of antagonist recalls Puff's Virtual Traumas about garbage trucks. In setting aside his preoccupation with food, he focuses on something that might be considered food's opposite. Although cats without pets, like Puff in her days on the street, often scrounge for meals in what humans consider garbage, I believe that in Slade's daydream a garbage truck is a garbage truck, not a fast-food stand.

The garbage itself symbolizes the felinemotional detritus of which Slade hopes to rid himself in catanalysis. Let us see where his trusty shades take him.

> When I opened my eyes I was in a tree outside the house. Faster than a speeding squirrel, I sailed through the air and landed—on my feet, what else?—on top of the monster's head. It roared that grinding roar again, and this time I caught what it

* This term has come down to us from Samuel T. Cateridge, who, with his fellow poet William Meowsworth, founded the Romanticat literary movement. Cateridge's best-known works, "The Rime of the Ancient Mouser" and "Kubla Kat," are still recited in kitten schools today.

said: "Fee, fie, foe, fat—I smell the fur of a mangy cat!"

This insult was too much. I had cleaned my fur just that morning, and not just a lick and a promise, either. I jumped down to the ground, picked up a twig, and barred the monster's path. Had to keep an eye out for its pets, though—letting them see me would bring disaster.

My twig turned into a sword, and one of those mouseketeer's hats showed up on my head. No, that's not right—I mean *mus*keteer's hats. Not the kind with the ears, the kind with the feather plumes. All for one and one for all, and like that.

I stared into one of the monster's glassy eyes and hissed, "Hey you! Out of this neighborhood!"

"Fat chance, Fluffy!" the monster shouted.

"You," I growled, "may call me 'Sir.' " Sword in paw, I got ready to attack.

Slade's struggle with the monster may well stand for what human analysts call the Oedipus complex. Whereas humans generally refer to the oedipal situation in a figurative sense, many cats can identify with Oedipus's rivalry with his father and attraction to his mother on a more literal level. (Recall, for example, Felix's brother Daddy, mentioned in Chapter 1.)

What humans call "incest" and consider taboo is known by the more benign term "inbreeding" when applied to higher species, but the emotions involved may nevertheless be powerful. One indication of Slade's antagonism toward his father is his fantasy of a hideous yellow monster in place of the undoubtedly pawsome tom who actually sired him.

Just then I heard the monster's pets stomping toward me. Launching myself into the air, I jumped back onto its yellow head just as the two humans climbed in and slammed its sides.

The monster moved along the street in fits and starts. In front of every house it stopped for another snack, and I began to think I would have to get tough.

Then suddenly it stumbled over a pothole, and I lost my grip on its scalp. I rolled head over tail, felt my hat and sword fall away, and ended up on the ground in front of the monster. Worst of all, one of its pets was staring right at me.

This was it—disaster! The human showed its stubby teeth in a grin and yelled, "Here, kitty kitty kitty!"

Lucky I've got a full-length fur coat, or the whole world would have seen me blush.

The good news was that the monster kept rolling along. When it finally disappeared around the corner, I heaved a purr of relief and declared the neighborhood a monster-free zone.

The psycatherapeutic value of catnip treatment is evident in Slade's efficient conversion of an everyday happening like trash collection to a Virtual Adventure—scarcely a hint of Daydreaming Dullness remains. And his developing confidence shows in his ability to face "disaster"—the human's recognition of his real identity—without succumbing to Virtual Trauma. Furthermore, his eventual nonviolent victory over the monster indicates a successful resolution of his oedipuss complex: vanquishing the symbolic father, he frees the neighborhood (as well as his own inner kitten) from garbage.

But let it not be said that Slade takes well-adjustedness to extremes. No gerbil he. The sword he wields with such flair obviously represents a compensatory fantasy for what he lost in undergoing the Operation. Humans, with their penchant for obscure jargon, call this a castration complex; we cats, more willing to call a spayed a spayed, use the simpler phrase "needing fixing after being fixed."*

An additional indication of Slade's feeling of loss is the musketeer's hat he wears into battle, with its feathers recalling Abby's plumelike tail. No doubt, comparing himself with his sister, he fears that his own tail, which resembles a pencil far more than a quill pen, marks him as in danger of, symbolically, being erased.†

My initial impression, as I read from the computer screen in the predawn hours, was that Slade's account ended with the monster-free zone. Just as I was about to close the file, however, I noticed an indication that the message continued. Once again I pounced on the computer's mouse, and the screen revealed a few more lines.

> I closed my eyes behind my shades—and this time when I opened them I was back in the good old window seat. Feeling just a tiny bit tense, I

* The low self-esteem resulting from this condition is often a factor in cases of catnip abuse: We call this "needing a fix after being fixed."

† See my "A Feather in His Cap: The Plumed Hat as a Fixation of Fixed Male Shorthairs," *Review of Compensatory Millinery* (1991).

jumped down to the floor for some stretching. Dug my claws into the oriental rug to get rid of any traces of the monster's scalp. Then I turned in a circle three times and curled up for a hard-earned nap. It had been a satisfying morning, no matter what color my dreams were about to be.

This final paragraph performs an important function. Reversing the transition from real life to healthy daydreaming, it returns Slade to the safety and comfort of his Good Home, a refuge from which he can go forth confidently in pursuit of further Virtual Adventures.

* * *

Before I present Abby's first e-mailed Virtual Adventure, let me mention another insight I gained from my work with the twins. With their catanalysis progressing electronically, I had no reason to pay them a visit for several weeks. Then one late-autumn day my cross-training program again took me near their window. At the sound of my voice they came to the window seat and purred a greeting.

I was amazed at the change in their appearance. Slade was sleek and muscular, with no trace of kitten fat, and Abby, as she bounded up to the window seat, seemed almost weightless beneath her glossy fur. Both were clearly several ounces lighter and considerably more energetic than at our earlier meetings. Their e-mail had shown their fantasies to be transformed; it seemed their bodies had undergone a transformation as well. The actual loss of weight accompanying their new low-calorie daydreams suggested that catnip had physical as well as mental benefits.

Even the subject matter of Slade's first post-treatment fantasy may be seen as an effective appetite-suppressant. Perhaps a symbolic discarding of food—in this case by turning it into garbage—is a necessary step toward weight loss. This insight, combined with others gleaned from both twins' e-mail transmissions, led me to experiment with a combination of catnip treatment and guided daydreaming as a therapy for feline eating disorders.

Thus began one of my most successful endeavors, the program that, as news of it has spread by meow of mouth, has come to be known as the Daydreaming Diet. My forthcoming book *Weight Loss the Winnicat Way* will make its benefits available to the general feline public.*

* In this project I am fortunate to have as a collaborator Dr. Walt Whitcat, best known for his verse treatise on a natural remedy for hairballs, *Leaves of Grass.* Also in the works is a collaborative effort with the celebrated chef Julia Kitten: a cookbook, *The Art of Feline Cooking,* based on the precepts of the Winnicat Way.

5

THE ABOMINABLE SNOWFLAKE

Abby's first transmission was just as low in calories—and just as adventurous—as Slade's. She entitled it "The Abominable Snowflake."

The October sun felt more like August. Our pets called it Indian summer. I was stretched out on my back in the window seat, wishing the pets would open the window and trying to think cool thoughts.

The pets were eating breakfast and reading the paper. "Sweetie," the smaller pet said, "this is interesting—a mountaineer claims he saw the Abominable Snowman in the Himalayas."

Her mate frowned. "I've got a problem with this World Series—I like both teams."

The smaller pet continued: "It says some people think The Abominable Snowman is really a large mountain cat."

The Himalayas. I've been told I look exactly like a Himalayan. My brother is just a plain gray shorthair, if you ask me, even if he does sometimes pretend to be a Russian Blue aristocat in exile. I licked a paw and wondered if the Himalayas had cooler weather.

I jumped down from the window seat and walked over to my carpet. The carpet is just the right size for a cat, and the blue in its pattern matches my eyes. I curled up on it, slipped my blue silk scarf around my neck—and closed my eyes.

Note that Abby, like Slade with his dark glasses, employs a mechanism that allows her to enter the Virtual world at will. Hers is twofold, involving both a carpet and a silk scarf.

While I have found no early writings linking our species to tinted eyeglasses, our relationship with fine carpets is a venerable one, going back at least as far as ancient Egypt. Consider the famous queen-in-the-carpet scene in Willie Shakestail's *Ratony and Cleopurrtra*, in which the Feline queen of Egypt and her high-ranking Rodent lover are defeated by the armies of the Rodent Empire.* And, as every educated feline knows, the phrase "as snug as a *bug* in a rug" originated in a misreading of the hieroglyph for "peerless cat" by a human Egyptologist (undoubtedly a Dog Person) who valued rhyme above accuracy.

We are associated with silk in history as well: An ancient custom of dressing cats in delicate silks, it is said, gave rise to the rather sweet human tendency to express approval by calling something "the cat's pajamas."†

* In another of Shakestail's plays the same Ratony asks his "friends, Rodents, countrymice" to lend him their ears. The loan he has in mind is a long-term one indeed, as Cleo considers Rodent ears a tasty snack.

† In what humans call the Victorian age, mention of anything as intimate as pajamas was forbidden; hence the euphemistic phrase "the cat's

When I opened my eyes my carpet and I were far above the ground. I had a sense of traveling a great distance.

At last the carpet came to rest. All around me the sun sparkled on snowy mountains, and I wished I had borrowed my brother's trusty shades.

My only firstpaw knowledge of snow came from times when our pets had rushed into the house brushing it from their clothes and stomping their feet to get it off their boots. I had heard the larger pet say some not very polite words after shoveling the sidewalk. Nothing in this beautiful bright landscape explained why snow made humans so irritable.

I stepped off the carpet—and sank. The snow swallowed me up.

I've always loved hiding in caves—a cardboard box, say, or the laundry basket. But being over my ears in icy white stuff definitely did not give me that same good feeling. I began to understand why the larger pet had used those words. Sneezing, I clawed my way out of the drift and clung to the crusty surface.

Then I heard a low, gravelly voice, as if the mountain itself were speaking: "Why do you think you have those double paws?" I spread my paws wide and, yes! they made perfect snowshoes. I must have been born to live in a place like this! I rushed off across the drifts, with my tail and my scarf billowing behind me.

Both Abby and Slade take commendable pride in their extra toes, which cats with small feet and match-

meow," which Queen Victoria herself, reportedly used to describe her beloved husband. What the palace cats thought of their royal pets has not been recorded.

ing minds have been known to ridicule. Polydactyly, I am convinced, is a step in the evolution of feline front paws into grasping organs like those of primates. The opposable thumb—with its promise of the independent wielding of can openers—is perhaps the only area in which cats have reason to aspire to be more like humans. When it is added to our ingenious retractable claws, we will have the whole world in our paws.

The reveries of both twins hint at a healthy appreciation of their own good looks. Plump or slender, *Felis catus* is a beautiful species, and we do well to rejoice in our own loveliness. Living in close proximity to the aesthetically challenged *Homo sapiens,* of course, makes our beauty all the more apparent.

I was pleased to read of Abby's eagerness for adventure. Although Slade has portrayed her hiding behind a houseplant, in her Virtual existence she plunges into exploration with all four feet. Her enthusiasm is particularly impressive after her experience of being swallowed by the snow.*

> I stopped in the shadow of a snowbank. But it wasn't a snowbank after all—it spoke! "Welcome, Kitten," said a voice like the low rumbling of an avalanche.
>
> "Who are you?" my meow squeaked.
>
> The answering voice made the snow tremble,

* This experience calls to mind the legend of a morose Middle Eastern shorthair named Jonah, who is said to have been eaten by a fish or a whale. Believing in such a stark reversal of the natural food chain requires a true pounce of faith.

and I trembled, too. "I am your great-great-great-great grandmama, give or take a few greats. Humans call me the Abominable Snowman—but as the proverb says, 'To err is human, to forgive feline.' "

The owner of the voice uncurled and stood up, balancing on two legs. Then she crouched to look me in the eye, and I could see she was a cat, a giant cat. Her eyes were the same bright gold as Slade's; otherwise, she looked very much like me. She even had double paws, each one larger than my whole body.

I spoke without thinking. "Grandma, what big feet you have!"

"They also call me Bigfoot," the great cat said, "and you can see why. It seems you have inherited my well-endowed paws."

I held out a paw for comparison. "You truly are my grandma?"

"Yes, Grandkitten. And you are named after me."

"But my name is Abby."

Her tail swept from side to side, brushing clouds of powdery snow into the air. "Abby is only your nickname. Do you remember when you first moved in with your pets, when you were no bigger than the dustballs under their bed?"

Now I was sure the giant cat was a member of our family—how else could she know about the pets' standards of housekeeping? Slade and I have spent many happy hours chasing dust kittens big enough to be our littermates.

"Well, you were a fierce little thing. Your pets would dangle toys in the air, and you would stand on two legs to attack. Your excellent posture made you resemble me. But you were too tiny for an Abominable Snowman, so your pets named you the

Abominable Snowflake instead. And called you Abby, for short."

I began to shiver—and not from the cold. The pets called me "abominable" whenever I stood on two legs to play. I knew this was not normally a compliment, and yet they seemed to intend it as one. Slade and I had always suspected they didn't know the meaning of the word.

At last I understood. "I like my name," I said.

Whereas Slade was concerned with so-called oedipal issues, involving conflict and its successful resolution, Abby's journey of discovery satisfies the longing to identify with something larger than oneself. Many of us in this age of catanomie and catalienation experience such longings; few, however, express them quite so literally as Abby does in imagining a forecat who is indeed an oversized version of herself.*

Bonding with this larger entity also gives Abby a feeling of connection to her own ancestral roots. The reproductive habits of our species make the longing for roots common among us: Except in carefully regulated catteries, it is indeed a wise kitten that knows its own father.

By now the sun was sinking behind the mountains, and even in my Himalayan coat I had begun to feel the cold. I was eager to tell Slade about our great-great-great-great grandmama.

* Humans show evidence of similarly literal longings: A prime example is the film *King Kong.*

"Grandma," I mewed, "I'm not sure how to get home. I came here on a carpet, but now I've lost it."

The rumbling voice was familiar now, and reassuring. "I'll take you to it, little one."

With a gentle tug at the back of my neck, the giant cat lifted me in her teeth, exactly the way my mama used to carry me. I had a sudden urge to purr. I did purr, quietly, during the short walk down the mountain, and felt strangely sad when she lowered me to the ground.

There was my carpet, pale blue against the mountainside. I stepped onto it, then turned to say farewell. But all I could see was snow, tinted rosy gold by the sunset.

"Good-bye, Grandma," I whispered—and closed my eyes.

When I opened them I was at home, looking out the window at Indian summer. I would have to think more cool thoughts. Slade was asleep at the other end of the window seat, and in the kitchen the pets were just finishing breakfast. Although the sun had set in the Himalayas, it was still morning here at home.

I needed a nap. Just a short one. Then I'd stand up on two legs, as Abominable as I could be, and wake my brother to tell him why we had double paws.

Abby's search for connection has taken her back to kittenhood. At the conclusion of the daydream she briefly regresses to infancy, secure in the care of a larger-than-life mamacat, and then is ready to face her own adult cathood.

Abby is in no more danger than Slade of being mistaken for a gerbil. Her search for her forecats may be a way to compensate for the feelings of loss resulting from her Operation: the loss of her chance to produce descendcats of her own.* She achieves a resolution of this ambivalence, however, and basks in the pleasure of her new insight into her ancestry. Her daydream ends with a return to the Good Home, as Slade's did, and in keeping with her theme of connection, the ending reaffirms her real-life bond with her twin.

Abby's fantasy, like Slade's, reveals a remarkable recovery from Daydreaming Dullness. After catnip treatment she dreams not about meals but, on the contrary, about vigorous activity—confirming my suspicion that catnip therapy plus guided daydreaming may provide a cure for feline obesity. Abby does not mention any appetite-suppressant corresponding to Slade's garbage, but perhaps all that calorie-free snow, combined with her high-altitude aerobic exercise, performs a similar function.

* * *

After perusing a few more e-mail messages from Abby and Slade, I judged it time to terminate their catanalysis. From Daydreaming Dullness the twins had rapidly progressed to rich Virtual Adventures—rich, that is, in felinemotional satisfaction, which nourishes the spirit

* What else she may feel she lost by undergoing the Operation is explored in a somewhat sensational manner in *Lady Catterley's Lover,* by the controversial British shorthair Fritz H. Lawrence.

without fattening the flesh. Unlikely to regress to devoting 98 percent of their fantasy lives to food, they were ready to stand on their own eight paws. Technically speaking, they had, both physically and felinemotionally, shed their excess baggage.

6

AD HOC, AD HOC, AND QUID PRO QUO

During the period in which I was receiving Abby and Slade's midnight messages I was also working with three patients who lived their *entire lives* in a daydream. They were triplets called Ad Hoc, Ad Hoc, and Quid Pro Quo (names I could not have invented). I assumed at first that the humans who had chosen these mysterious monickers must be Latin scholars. But one of the three—I believe it was either Ad Hoc or Ad Hoc—explained that he and his brothers had been named after a line in a film, something to do with a Nowhere Man and four human musicians who, in a curious combination of flawed spelling and insect-envy, called themselves Beatles.

Franz Catka, the moody European tabby who in *Metamousosis* imagines becoming an oversized bug, is the only one of our own species, so far as I am aware, who has shown any sign of insect-envy. But humans, of course, might understandably be envious of any number of their fellow creatures.

The idea of the insect as meta-mouse, by the way, has

aroused controversy ever since *Metamousosis* first appeared. Not surprisingly, the most rabid attacks on this concept have spread from the rodent community, while the few insects who venture to participate in mammalian scholarly discourse are stinging in its support. The feline consensus is best captured in the philosophical precept "If it moves, pounce on it."

After arduous research involving the use of the remote control on my pets' TV set to watch old films,* I tracked down the names of my patients. In an animated film entitled *The Yellow Submarine*, a character called the Nowhere Man dashes around chanting "Ad hoc, ad hoc, and quid pro quo—so little time, so much to know!"

This discovery prompted me to inquire whether the triplets had been the only kittens in their litter. At first they insisted they had, but after I quoted the Nowhere Man they began to recall two sisters named Little and Much—nicknames, so they said, for So Little Time and So Much to Know. (Dr. Furrenczi has asserted that I elicited the memory of Little and Much by suggestion. I can only reply that anything elicited by suggestion from *me* must surely be good for my patients.)

The brothers told me that their pet humans belonged to a socially challenged generation known as Boomers (a term usually modified by the word *Baby*, indicating

* Regrettably, cats have not been consulted about the design of remote controls: The buttons are so small as to be almost impossible to manipulate with a paw. The computer, in contrast, must have been invented by felinengineers; the transformation of the mouse from basic food group to electronic cat's-paw shows a genius far beyond the human.

that this generation of humans is expected to remain immature). The Boomers' formative years had coincided with the fame of the Beatles and other musical groups with names such as Stones, Who, Monkees, and Dead.

This list provides a wealth of material for speculation—*Who* must be a symptom of a profound crisis of identity; *Monkees* reveals still more cross-species envy, once again combined with an inability to spell the envied name correctly; while *Stones* implies a self-image so low that the humans envy inanimate (though often described as *Rolling*) objects. And speaking of things inanimate, the interpretation of the name *Dead,* most often coupled with the adjective *Grateful,* I leave to cat-analysts more philosophically inclined than I.*

* * *

The triplets first scratched at my cat door while I was in a catanalytic session with Puff. Interruption of a session, for any reason short of physical danger (as in the case of Felix's attack on my ear—see Chapter 1), is inadvisable, but lacking a receptioncat I was forced to respond myself.

I pushed open the door with my nose and saw three identical young black cats, thin to the point of emaciation, staring at me with identical anxious expressions.

* Another oddly named group, the Lovin' Spoonful, recorded a song entitled "Daydream" that could be a motto for my practice. "What a day for a daydream," it begins, "what a day for a daydreaming [cat]." See my "A Spoonful of Catnip Helps the Daydreaming Go Down," in *Best Felinessays of 1992* (Pushcat Press, 1993).

Postponing the traditional sniffing, I asked them to wait outside under a dogwood tree.

After Puff's session I found my new patients carving designs in the bark of the tree with their claws (they were in no danger: As feline scientists have proved conclusively, a dogwood's bark is worse than its bite). I escorted them into my office and retrieved two grocery bags from the pantry to add to the one just vacated by Puff.

I asked the patients to introduce themselves, and the one in the leftmost bag answered: "This is my brother Ad Hoc, you can call him Addie, and this is my brother Ad Hoc, you can call him Hoc, and I'm their brother Quid Pro Quo, you can call me Quid. We're on a real downer, Doc. It's like, we can't get no satisfaction."

This plea for satisfaction aroused my curiosity.* I wondered if perhaps the triplets had been subjected to the Operation without being informed of its inevitable effects.

Quid continued: "It's like a hard rain's a gonna fall, cuz the times they are a'changin', and baby won't light our fire, so we'll all live in a yellow submarine in an octopus's garden in the shade."

The brothers, it seemed, imagined themselves living beneath a body of water, in close proximity to a large, horticulturally inclined mollusk. Unaware, at the time,

* Curiosity is rumored to be fatal, but daydreaming, of the guided type I have pioneered in my practice, is an ideal way of exercising it in safety. In a Virtual setting, curiosity kills no cats.

of the derivation of their names from a submarine movie, I interpreted this as straightforward Virtual Trauma. It called to mind the biblical story of the Deluge, but without the hope offered by the animal-rescue pioneer named Noah and the floating shelter he called the Ark.

My initial diagnosis was Daydream Misdirection, the affliction for which I had treated Puff (Chapter 2). Queries about the triplets' daydreams, however, elicited answers indistinguishable from those to questions about their daily lives. I gradually realized that they perceived the entire world from within a shared daydream.

For example, when I asked how they had spent the previous afternoon, not one of their replies was appropriate to their own decade or even to their own species. Addie described sitting in at an army recruiting office, Hoc mentioned playing ultimate Frisbee at a love-in, and Quid told of a political rally at which he and thousands of others had yowled "Impeach Nixon!" Reality could not penetrate this pathological nostalgia: These three brothers, born in the nineties, had no idea that the sixties were long over.

* * *

To account for their affliction I must relate a bit more background. Addie, Hoc, and Quid's pet humans were Boomers named Darin and Dee, who pursued successful careers as professors of Postdeconstructionist Renovationism (Darin) and Tax Loopholes (Dee, whose specialty was White-Collar Crime) at universities near Boston.

The life of a human university professor, like that of a cat, allows considerable latitude in appearance and behavior. Darin and Dee, when the triplets entered their lives, dressed and behaved much as they had in their undergraduate days in the sixties. Darin, for example, taught his classes barefoot, in bell-bottom trousers and an embroidered shirt, and with a beaded headband around what he called his Irish Afro.

Dee, whose position at a prestigious business school required her to follow a fashion known as Dress for Success, asserted her flower-child identity by wearing peace-symbol earrings (created exclusively for her in gold and platinum), accessorizing her designer suits with scarves of tie-dyed silk, and sporting a license plate reading WOODSTOCK on her BMW. At home she peeled off her pantyhose, discarded her underwire bras in favor of T-shirts with slogans like "Make love, not war," and played digital reissues of old LP's at top volume while doing step aerobics.

Darin and Dee had met when both, if I may borrow a phrase from Boomer dialect, "tuned in, turned on, and dropped out" to join an organization called Hare Krishna. As I understand it, adherents of this sect wear robes the color of the paler stripes of ginger tabbies (not an unappealing shade, but far more attractive on the originals than on these literal copycats), shave off much of their naturally sparse human fur, and spend long hours chanting a few phrases over and over.

The grandmama of Quid and the Ad Hocs* was born in the Hare Krishna ashram and grew to catolescence there. When Dee, bored with the sect's repetitive lyrics, achieved enlightenment in the form of a vision of a golden tax loophole arching across the heavens, and resolved to follow it to the ends of the earth, yea, even unto an M.B.A.; and when Darin experienced a revelation that a woman so deeply in tune with her inner tycoon as to hitch her wagon to a golden loophole was exactly the companion with whom he wished to travel the yellow brick road of life, and that while she went back to school to study White-Collar Crime he might as well get a degree in something modern and up to date, or better yet postpostpostmodern and at the cutting edge, so that in later years while she brought home the bacon he could make a career of splitting hairs, or to maintain the culinary image, of slicing the angel-hair pasta . . .

Where was I? At times, I fear, my prose echoes the speech patterns of patients whose catnip dosage has been imperfectly calibrated. When, as I was saying, the young human couple underwent this spiritual transformation, they took with them to their new life—or what they called their new lifestyle—the young female cat whom the Krishnas had astutely called The Unnameable

* Or should the plural be Ads Hoc, or perhaps Ad Hocii? Classicats please respond. Although I am fluent in several ancient languages, including Saber-Tooth Tiger and Ur-Cat, the much younger languages *humans* consider ancient have not been part of my education.

One, but on whom Darin and Dee bestowed the name Dow Jones.

* * *

The renowned felineurologist Dr. Oliver Bags has treated cats suffering from damage to the brain due to disease or to trauma such as that inflicted by canine jaws. One of his patients, a male in middle cathood, shared Addie, Hoc, and Quid's penchant for quoting songs from the sixties. His memories, like theirs, were frozen in an earlier time: Because of a brain tumor, he remembered nothing since his catolescence. In the case of Dow Jones's kittens and grandkittens, however, the felineurological problems arose from something quite different, a danger of which all so-called domesticated cats should beware: *too close an identification with their human pets*.

Hints of how this destructive process operated have already appeared in the history of Darin and Dee. In their post–Hare Krishna lives they clung to outward signs of their hippie youth, but their new priorities were revealed by their career choices and the name they assigned to the erstwhile Unnameable One. The internal tension between their nostalgia and their professional and financial aspirations demanded resolution, and they resolved it, most ingeniously if inadvertently, by displacing the nostalgia onto Dow Jones's daughter Eleanor Rigby, and later onto Eleanor's kittens Ad Hoc, Ad Hoc, and Quid Pro Quo.

The triplets suffered from a rare condition I have

labeled *Displaced Daydreaming:* They were trapped in fantasies not their own. Thus they followed a vegetarian diet (the cause of their life-threatening emaciation), irritated local tomcats by responding to traditional threats with nonviolent resistance, marched four-footedly in demonstrations for causes known only to themselves, called their Good Home a commune, and reminisced about past lives in which they had been humans or other lower beings.

* * *

When I proposed catnip therapy, all three brothers professed their enthusiasm—or so I interpreted their "Like wow!" As I sprinkled the herb on the couch, Quid bit off a fragment of his paper bag, brushed a small mound of catnip onto it with his paw, and rolled it into a cylinder. "Got a light?" he asked.

"What do you have there?" I replied neutrally. "A catnip cigarette?"

"Call it whatever you want," Quid answered. "But hey, if it looks like a joint, and quacks like a joint, I say we smoke it."

I have always opposed mixing fire with fur. Even singed whiskers can be a serious disability, and once the coat has begun to smolder the danger of fatality is high. Thus, on the theory that where there's smoke there's fire,* I am against feline smoking.

* This theory has been attributed to Dr. Furrenczi. If indeed it is his, I consider it his most original contribution to scientific thought.

Catnip, fortunately for my career, is a drug that exerts its effects without being ignited. Quid's request for a light was merely a figure of meow; when I ignored it, he inhaled deeply of the fragrance of the herb, then passed the "joint" to one of his brothers. The session was largely silent, except for an occasional purred "Groovy!" from one Ad Hoc or another, until the roll of catnip returned to Quid and he pushed it toward me.

"Toke, Doc?"

"Not while I'm on duty." (This automatic response came from my reading of what humans call mystery novels. In that genre, the human detectives spend their time refusing alcoholic beverages offered by murder suspects, leaving the cats to sniff out clues, stalk perpetrators, and get their teeth into the evidence.)

"S'okay," Quid said, "but watch out for the contact high."

By this time the Ad Hocii were tussling on my couch as they competed for the cigarette. Quid passed it to them, then licked a few loose shreds of the herb off the couch, flattening the nap of the fabric with his tongue.

For me, the moment was one of epiphany. Quid's offpaw comment revealed to me, in a burst of insight, the origin of his malady. If the catnip "joint" had been lit, I might have caught a contact high simply from being in the room with the smokers. In much the same way, Addie, Hoc, and Quid had caught their fixation on the sixties simply from being exposed to their pets' nostalgia. If I may quote Felix's brother Daddy (Chapter 1), they had listened to humans too much.

* * *

Addie, Hoc, and Quid remain in catanalysis at this writing. For some time they continued to take the medication in the form of paw-rolled cigarettes, but as their attachment to the sixties weakened they began to sniff the herb directly from the cushion in the normal fashion.

The one major setback in their treatment underscores the lesson to be learned from their affliction. It is a sad truth that we cats, in our domestic alliance with humans, risk being overinfluenced by their species. Trends in human society affect us in serious and unpredictable ways. For example, just when Addie, Hoc, and Quid had begun to talk in seventies lyrics (I would cite some lyrics here, but having found them far less memorable than those of the sixties, I cannot recall any) and to swing their tails in a rhythm they called Disco—the first stage of recovery, one decade at a time—human trendwatchers declared a sixties revival, and the patients regressed.

I am confident, however, that in time the triplets will cease to "turn on and tune in" and will learn to tune *out* Darin and Dee's daydreams in order to dream their own. In a recent session one of the Ads Hoc, his tail arched in an expression of utter seriousness, asked me if Elvis Presley had truly married the Jackson Five. This confusion of decades is only a beginning, but it encourages me to predict a complete cure. My official prognosis: Their recovery is in the bag.

7

THE CASE OF THE MISSING MITTENS

The most controversial question in catanalytic circles today concerns whether to offer catnip therapy to kittens. The psycatpharmacological treatment of the young has caused more hissing, spitting, and even paw-to-paw combat than any other catanalytic issue of our time.*

Kittens, all the combatants agree, are born with a talent for fantasy play. According to the anti-drug forces, no circumstances can justify biochemical tinkering with the daydreams of patients young enough to retain this inborn ability.

But how young is young enough? Any inborn ability is subjected, from the moment of birth, to the bites and scratches of outrageous fortune. A kitten's flair for playful daydreaming is especially vulnerable to disorders of the *parents'* fantasy lives. Thus in certain cases a parent's disorder (usually that of the mamacat, as in feline society the two-parent family is a custom most honored

* See my "Pussycat or Pusherman?" *Kittenhood Today* (June 1994). And for an opposing view see, if you must, Dr. Furrenczi's "The Katnip Konspiracy," *Feline Family Values Forum* (August 1994).

in the breach) may call for catnip treatment of the kittens. For a clear example, let me recount the story of a trio of small felines who appeared in my office one day with their mamacat.

* * *

Taffy (not her real name) was a calico shorthair, while her babies, a little tom and his two sisters, showed promise of luxurious long black-and-white fur. Taffy was in her late catolescence, perhaps too young to face the responsibility of a family—and indeed, she informed me that this was her first litter. The stress was obvious in her angry, slitted eyes, and in the incessant jerky motion of her tail. The kittens themselves revealed little purrsonality, appearing subdued and sleepy.

When I guided them toward the usual grocery bag, one of the youngsters mewed, "Mama, what's the sack for?" I consider myself something of a semanticat, but until that moment I had not noticed that some speakers of Felinenglish say "sack" rather than "bag." If the technical terminology of catanalysis had developed within this linguistic tradition, I wondered, would we declare a cured patient "sacked out" instead of "out of the bag"? At the end of treatment, would we sack the patient? or vice versa? I contemplated composing a letter to the editor of the *American Catanalytic Journal*, or better yet *The Mew York Times.*

The kittens settled together in one bag, Taffy in another. All four gazed at me in silence for so long that I was tempted to quote that most prolific of rodent au-

thors, Anonymouse, and ask if the cat had got their tongues. Instead, I inquired how I could be of help.

When Taffy finally spoke, her meow was shrill and staccato, and the pulsing of her tail accelerated.

> It started when they ran up to me crying "Mother Dear, see here, see here." They never call me Mother Dear unless they're in trouble. This time, the little scamps had lost their mittens. I knitted those mittens myself, I'll have you know. Stayed up long past my naptime day after day, working my poor paws to the bone.
>
> How could they be so careless? I've brought them up to take care of their things. When I was their age I never had anything of my own—just paw-me-downs from my mama's older litters.
>
> I blame it on Prince—that's their daddycat. They look just like him, but he's never laid eyes on them, never sent one bite of kitten support. You'd think he could cough up a few mouthfuls of sparrow or squirrel now and then.

She looked at me expectantly, but in proper cat-analytic style I coughed up no words, let alone anything edible. Then her tone changed, and for a moment a smile made her whiskers quiver.

> He's a fiddler, used to play down at the Hey Diddle Diddle—the pawsomest tomcat I'd ever seen, and his licks could make cows jump over the moon. To me he was a dream come true.
>
> I should have known it was only fur-deep. When we met he said he wanted as many kittens as pos-

sible—then when I got pregnant he made like the Cheshire cat and faded away. I tried to find him after these three were born, but he'd changed his name and left town.

I know what you'll say, it's always been this way,* a tom's gotta do what a tom's gotta do. But Doctor, this single mamahood is no kittycats' picnic! More like the myth of Sisypuss, if you ask me.†

She rubbed a paw across her face as if brushing off the memories, then spat at her progeny: "Lost your mittens? You naughty kittens! Now you shall have no pie!" Huddled in the holding environment they called a sack, the three little kittens began to cry.

* * *

Taffy's outburst aroused my concern. Her babies' paws sported the normal endowment of fur and had no need for clothing; the layered look has never caught on as a feline fashion. I suspected, in any case, that the mittens were more Virtual than real.

Her choice of punishment was further evidence of

* Taffy is correct here about feline tradition: In ancient languages such as Ur-Cat, the combination of sound and tail gesture meaning "daddy-cat" also meant "Now you see him, now you don't."

† Sisypuss, according to myth, was condemned to carry a large, wriggling rat up a steep hill over and over: Each time he reached the peak and opened his jaws to announce his success, the rat escaped and ran back to the bottom. A similarly arduous mythological task was the cleaning of the Augean litterbox. The designated cleaner, a hairless Greek-Belgian fat cat named Hercules Poirot, also performed other labors, many of them related to the solving of crimes.

confusion: As any rational mamacat knows, kittens are not, in general, fond of pie. Depriving them of salmon or chicken would have been far more effective.

Like the Ad Hocs and Quid Pro Quo, Taffy had trouble distinguishing her fantasy life from reality; unlike them, she was trapped not in human daydreams but in her own. And just as Addie, Hoc, and Quid's disorder resulted from the strong influence of their pet humans, Taffy's three little kittens were suffering from the influence of their mama's fantasies.

Little Wynken, Blynken, and Nod (not their real names, but expressive of their drowsy appearance) were disoriented and apprehensive because Taffy, bitter toward their absent daddycat and perceiving her own skewed Virtual world as real, tried to keep them warm and safe with imaginary mittens rather than with the holding and cuddling all kittens need. Because of her confusion, they did not feel secure enough to play: hence their lethargy. A kitten without play is like a catanalyst without patients, uncertain of its purpose in life.

I recommended twice-a-week family sessions, but Taffy informed me that one visit would have to suffice: She and her youngsters were taking to the road in search of the tomcatting musician formerly known as Prince. I would have preferred to continue treatment at least long enough to determine whether the fiddler was any more real than the mittens. (I did recall hearing about a cat from the Hey Diddle Diddle—some scandal involving a dish, a spoon, and a laughing canine.)

* * *

In the pre-catnip era I could have done little for these patients in one session, but the medication gave me some hope. I took the radical step of prescribing it not for the mamacat but for her litter.* Taffy's disorder, I reasoned, was too complex to respond to one-time treatment, but if I could induce the kittens to wake up and smell the catnip they might be able to pull her out of her Dysfunctional Daydreams to the benefit of the entire family unit.†

One minute dose of the drug—calibrated for their tiny bodies—made a tremendous difference in the kittens' energy level. Wynken immediately climbed my office curtains, Blynken knocked over a wastebasket, while Nod assassinated the mouse of my pets' computer. After these dramatic moments, however, the session calmed down and became one of the most satisfying of my career.

I offered each of the now wide-awake triplets a toy mouse made of cloth lightly scented with catnip. This was the *transitional mousie,* something all feline infants

* This course, of course, caused catcalls from colleagues; our exchange of views was reported somewhat disrespectfully by Hunter G. Thomcat in "Alley Catanalysts: Yowling Insults over the Shrinks' Back Fence," *Catlantic Monthly* (1994).

† I understand that a recent trend in human medicine called Managed Care encourages such a short-term approach to treatment, and that under its rules practitioners readily prescribe drugs for young patients. Can it be that catnip has been crooning in the Managers' ears?

need as they begin to differentiate themselves from their mamacat and their littermates.

After an adorable interlude of killing and rekilling their mousies, the kittens were ready for some family role-playing. At my prompting, Taffy growled at them about their allegedly missing mittens and declared they should have no pie. Instead of beginning to cry, however, they replied with a retort I had suggested, a quotation attributed to a human called Ben Franklin (his real name, insofar as he himself was real).* "The cat in gloves," they chanted, "catches no mice."

Note that this reply did not address the question of whether the kittens had ever, in reality, worn mittens. My strategy was to avoid that issue by convincing Taffy that her little ones would do better in life without their supposedly mislaid outerwear. One lesson catnip teaches us, if we listen with both ears, is that *the difference between fantasy and reality does not always matter.*

* * *

As the kittens overcame their fear of her scoldings, Taffy visibly relaxed. Her tail ceased its restless motion; her

* It is not Franklin's existence itself that is in question, but his claim to certain accomplishments. The witty sayings he published in *Poor Richard's Almanack* are now known to have been composed by "Poor" Richard himself, a Manx who slept by Franklin's fireside. The inadequate warmth generated by the fireplace prompted Richard to invent what has come to be known as the Franklin Stove. See "Richard and Poor Ben," in *Revolutionary American Shorthairs*, volume 12 of The Founding Felines series.

eyes opened to their full roundness. She also recovered from her mitten fixation, and by the end of the session she had promised that her offspring should have some pie.

I forbore to suggest an alternative treat. Taffy's budding confidence prompted me, in turn, to trust her mothering instincts. What kittens need, as I have long argued, is not a perfect mamacat but a *good-enough mamacat;* the catanalyst's task is to foster the mamacat's sense of her own good-enoughness. Surely, I now believed, Taffy had in mind not the usual apple or cherry pie but something like a nicely browned salmon quiche. (Although few of us crave pie, real cats do eat quiche.)

It was time to end the session. As the trio of small felines emerged from their bags, Taffy licked each one around the ears. Once outside my cat door, the kittens, abandoning their well-bitten transitional mousies, turned pawsprings and played leapcat on the lawn. Had I chosen pseudonyms for them based on their post-catnip behavior, my choices would have been not Wynken, Blynken, and Nod but perhaps Ready, Set, and Go.

Taffy lingered a moment to ask if I did couples counseling, "just in case I get my claws into His Royal Exness." She would not worry about mittens anymore, she confided shyly, because the catnip treatment had fitted her three little kittens like a glove.

CONCLUSION

As mamacats since saber-tooth days have crooned to their litters at weaning time, all good things must come to an end. And as my own kitten-school teachers used to say when I was reluctant to leave the fictional world of my favorite author,* all good *books* must come to an end. Let me bring this one to a close with a few words about the place of catnip in catanalysis.

To those who have learned to listen, catnip not only speaks but sings. Even the aurally acute, however, disagree about what they hear: some interpret the herb's serenade as the music of the spheres, others as a siren song enticing our profession toward fatal shores.

Having listened closely to both catnip and its opponents, I can testify that the former sings a better song. Above all, it sings of the power of the feline imagination. The classic insult heard whenever newly acquainted toms vie for status—"You lap cat!"—loses its bite when

* The author was the famous British longhair Dickens, whose drama of doomed littermates, *A Tale of Two Kitties*, was at the top of my list. I also devoured the coming-of-age novel *David Coppercat*, the psycatlogical thriller *Bleak Mouse,* and the poignant story of an orphaned stray, *Oliver Twisted Whiskers.*

every lap cat can battle monsters or travel through space and time.* There is no such thing as "just a housecat" when housebound felines can roam the Virtual world at will. Daydreams make the difference—and catnip, in many cases, makes the daydreams.

Furthermore, in contrast with traditional catanalysis, *Nepeta cataria* confers its benefits with impressive speed. Abby and Slade's fantasies evolved from dull to daring after only three doses of the herb, and one dose transformed Puff's Virtual Traumas into Virtual Adventures. Felix was in treatment somewhat longer, but he was my first catnip patient and I had much to learn. Addie, Hoc, and Quid, it is true, may need even lengthier catanalysis and more medication before they learn that although the Virtual realm is a fantastic place to visit, they do not actually live there. As for Taffy and her three little kittens, one tiny dose was enough to vanquish family-fragmenting mitten mania and pie deprivation.

It remains to be seen what these successes portend for our profession. Will catnip bring about radical changes in the venerable but often lengthy "meowing cure"? Will our descendcats take for granted the ability to fine-tune their daydreams with medication? Will the new catnippian music make Papa Sigmund roll over and play dead in his grave?

Catnip is the rising star on today's catanalytic stage,

* In any case, this old insult may evolve into a nostalgic term as laptop computers compete with our species for the limited supply of human laps. Already catanalysts report many patients suffering from laptop jealousy.

and like any star, it loves an audience. The more attentively we listen—whether through Dr. Furrenczi's headphones, through Dr. Jung's collective ear, or from the front row of the balcony—the more encores it will sing. It is time for catanalysts everywhere to stop pussyfooting around and learn to dance as catnip calls the tune.

ABOUT THE AUTHORS

SIGMUND F. WINNICAT (who uses his middle initial only, never the full name Fluffy) is best known for his fur-raising treatise on the malaise of modern feline society, *Domestication and Its Discontents*. He is also the author of *I'm a Cat, You're a Cat* and *Stroking Your Inner Kitten*. His forthcoming works include *Weight Loss the Winnicat Way* and *The Man Who Mistook His Wife for a Cat*. Dr. Winnicat lives in Massachusetts, in a Good Home with a cat door that allows him to see his patients.

CAMILLE SMITH is a senior editor at a publishing house in Cambridge, Massachusetts. She lives near Cambridge with her husband, Forrest Forque, and five of Dr. Winnicat's patients.